golden
mickey finn

for K.

i don't know if You'll ever read this. i don't know if You're dead or alive, or, if You are alive, whether You'll live long enough to see it in print. i don't know if You exist at all. but this is for You.

table of contents

i.   *introduction*
ii.   *quote*

1. on writing—
2. souls
3. just maybe
4. about dying
5. new phone
6. colours in the night
7. the fine game of nil
8. love
9. bodies
10. astronomical twilight
11. one time
12. safety
13. the three alcoholics
14. heebie's basement
15. toilet
16. optimism for the modern age
17. the prostitutes of sheil road
18. black umbrellas
19. these days
20. into pieces
21. late
22. look up (you're being lied to)
23. bubbles
24. high enough
25. americans
26. dreamers
27. everything is boring
28. stand up (the truth)

29. the system (i)
30. the system (ii)
31. the heart
32. smoking kills
33. blindfolds
34. divine
35. eclipse
36. die later
37. birdshit
38. fishing
39. christmastime and other bleak periods
40. don't come crying to us
41. luckies are less irritating
42. jillboots can kill a man
43. all you need know
44. stones
45. fuck you
46. before the devil knows i'm dead
47. old thoughts and new thoughs
48. trash
49. on equal fuckings
50. alpha
51. opium
52. lol
53. title: wewwo.mfvcnw page: one hundred and eight
54. cracks

56. the war

57. all that glitters
58. sitting outside
59. bombs
60. life and soul of the party
61. here
62. boiling frogs
63. live longer
64. until my head falls off
65. fuck you, too
66. come friendly robots
67. da da da da da
68. the theory of everything
69. acne
70. gilet jaunes
71. K, answer
72. fairytale
73. lost angeles
74. in tongues
75. the drink
76. umbra
77. softcore
78. allegory
79. hardcore
80. pornography
81. mum
82. i don't know
83. hypernormalisation
84. bleach
85. picture
86. wanker
87. Your dog
88. –poetry
89. in storms

introduction

the story begins here, with my never wanting to write it. i was quite content with two hundred of my inconsequential poems being read by two hundred and fifty thousand people across the world. the odd like or comment on a quickly eroding poetry website gave me all the dopamine hits i needed, even if the hit came while i spent yet another evening held up in my six foot by eight foot room, floating in my own sadness in perpetuity. i did not mind; i liked the noises in my head being *my* noises in *my* head, and i still do. i did not mind feeling the slow rot eat my stillness, and i still don't. the idea of any dream i ever had coming true was stabbed repeatedly, and i now don't know what to believe anymore.

but the increasingly overbearing, stale bubblegum taste of each new unimpressive zeitgeist would only ever force that to change, twinned with a painfully bitter heartbreak and various other gnawing frustrations i needed to try to and purge (which ultimately proved futile). then friends smarter than i am read my works and saw something in them; they suggested i use my *talent* to go places. they always resented the waste i am. i begrudge them for convincing me that my failed suicide attempts should count for something.

they were right, of course—even if the places to which i journeyed almost made it third time lucky; the scratching in my head had to get out. the three years spent unemployed teaching myself how to read, write, spell, and becoming an autodidact needed an end. writing golden prevented me from burrowing out from within my own skull. it provided that end. i tried and failed, for year after year, to write something that never led me to cross the road without looking, something that would stop me designating my pockets for certain possessions. the strangling normality was wringing me tighter, and i needed to either escape it entirely or willed it killed me. this is the first work that afforded me that breathing space; even then it only glances the philosophies and the qualities of the creeping spectre of postmodernism, and it's all through the eyes of a deluded, thoughtful waster, with too much to say to anybody apathetic enough to listen. and i have the gall to deem it readable, when even i can't tell if it's real. ha!

golden is the pixelated, true and false collection of poems which tells the story of when i met the love of my life, K, (who used the pseudonym 'golden' on the forum on which we both met). she is a woman who saved me without knowing she did, and our relationship exploding into life before breaking rapidly after a few blissful months of us being inseparable. this resulted in me reacquainting myself to the familiar, self-destructive isolation, having thought i had, at last, escaped it though K. consequently, i started to pick holes in those surroundings whilst simultaneously losing grip of something i always felt i had under my control. that is until she unexpectedly reappeared, and with her, her harbour, her safety, her power, her life-giving breaths, an escape from it all.

this resuscitation, however, was fleeting. i found myself in the deep end once more, which again resulted in a redoubling of the unpleasant bewilderment i felt the first time it happened. paired with agitation, the feelings only become further entrenched. i, at this point, wished to blow a hole in society and everything in it, or squeeze myself out of the collective puss. i wanted to escape—come hell or high water—from what i saw as an emptiness invading society, and the occupied growing to love their occupier. panaceas are a myth, but when she returned and i convinced myself of her being as such, the inevitable loss happened again; the abyss only looked at me harder.

what's left after i burned the pillars i relied on? what happens when you spit on the ashes of the institutions you once believed? who is the target and where does the gun turn when all society is dead? myself. the only real thing i really had with any certainty was myself. but i grew to bitterly hate that certainty the longer i spent time alone with it. the lonely times only got worse with each new rejection, each new false hope, each new desperate attempt to prove that all things aren't all bad. and… i snapped. i kicked out at the world, hoping it would kick back so i could at least be certain of something; i did not know what was real or fake (i still don't), let alone that the world couldn't give a shit who kicked it; being ignorant to the fact that i was my only world, which made everything worse. i hated myself, and now i ache after that kicking only hit me. not even my own thoughts were safe at that time. i questioned all i ever was, all i ever created, all i ever destroyed—anything that had ever happened to anybody i thought i knew.

all this, and my failed attempts of escaping, now leave me gutted and not knowing which way to turn. is love anything more than a chemical formula? is K real? i don't know. all i can do is hope; nothing can take hope away from me.

that remains true post-story.

"hope is the fuel of progress and fear is the jail in which you put
yourself."—tony benn

on writing

writing is like
talking to yourself,
except people don't
think you're crazy—

souls

last night, our souls
ended all

we took history by the collar
and kissed it into a bloody
knotted ruin

we severed our bodies
and transcended spacetime
beyond the barricades of light

we became death
destroyer of worlds,
dead
and resurrected

we were canonised,
baptised in the immortal, golden fires
of our sinful
mortal desires

our fusion erupted
a periodic table,
elements of the metaphysical
hunted by those
misguided people
who scramble after what they think
love is

we know their scratches
on the surface of our duvet
are smooth and simply
chemical, because
we tied ourselves up in it
and fell apart,
lost everything but

one another,

and that was the moment when,
if i had plucked it
from time,
from the fabric of life—
when humanity was
closest to heaven—
it was then,
when we tore down the universe
with our naked,
bleeding
souls.

just maybe

maybe
You and i
should take off our shoes
and swirl around the golden
shore's dunes
as they whistle,
skin in bone
home from home,
taken by the sunlight
You blacken.

maybe we should follow our
love
into the waves,
feel their warmth lap
against our shoulders,
letting them purify us

maybe
we should walk
until our feet
don't touch the bottom;

maybe,
just maybe,
i could save Your life
that way.

about dying

You said
we should die together
grow yellow with drink,
just decide to end it all
one day,
go out in our own way
on our own time
just the two of us
after we're finished
chasing memories
we're yet to make

i told You countless times
about my love for You
and meant it
for the first
time,
every
time

and i died,
each time
too

and i don't know about You
but i think that, now
we're both dead
in our own chains
our own caves;

we just never chose how.

new phone

i got a new phone today—

figured i'd treat myself,
try that retail therapy
i've heard so much about

it's new, and shiny,
and its button is
a perfect circle, and it loads
my life up
point five seconds faster
than the piece of shit
i overpaid for
last year

then i tried to transfer
the pictures of You, the woman
i once loved
just so that i could
look at them
from time to time,
filterless and
unforgivingly golden
pretending
the love i still have
is justified

but they all went away

just like You.

colours in the night

i ripple in prussian blue
i inhale the night's puncture wounds
the tiny
circular ponds
looking for
You,
spiralling off
between worried
shades of asbestos grey

spiralling
away
away
away,

Your amber smile
away
Your fireworks
away
the angels and the demons
i see in Your eyes
away

it's pitch black
in the cave
now You've set

i hope You circle back around
and rise again
soon

just don't go
don't go.

the fine game of nil

the world is a world of tears
and the burden of our mortality
cuts the heart

release the fear

release the idea of worth
we're worthless, and
You're just specks of dust that determine
the fate of the cosmos—
vesuvian ash,
nothing more than a player
in the fine game of nil
on the field that defines the rules—
the spreading universe—
like ecru frost circles
on stained glass windows
when the volcanic plumes
blot out the sun again.

You played,
You played the fine game with me
when we sat in hollows by gaslight, golden
finally warm

but i lost
and now i've got a touch of
cotard's delusion
and i need Your soul's teeth
to scrape the dead layers off once more,
like You did before the cries
of each lost generation
stopped.

the burden of mortality cuts the heart

and the world is a world of tears,
tears we lose in the rain.

love

love, the only
sensation that gifts
the strength required
to reduce mountains
to dust
with your bare hands
whilst, at the same time,
grinding you
into the cold, forsaken dirt
the very moment
it takes hold.

bodies

bodies eternally
rot;
they are borrowed,
but the mind can
live forever
so long as you
cultivate it.

water yourself.

astronomical twilight

i don't want words
to spoil this drive
this nostalgia
of places i long for,
of homes
i don't know exist,
of paired major and
minor chords
melancholic winds
humming
on the quiet
coastal roads
cutting through the gentle
benighted dusk.

nobody cares
and i'm glad

as visuals lead the way
they take me back
to my hypnogogia

my unfurling as liquid,
uncontainable,
underappreciated

i'm not happy
or sad,
i'm just
unplugged.

one time

never forget the morning
when you got a cab
back from the city
and stopped it early
because you thought
the alcohol and motion
was making you sick.

never forget collapsing
onto the freshly cut grass and
the dead, dry heaps
the council leave lying around
to blow off to any damn place
the wind pleases.

it's just outside your house
and you sat and watched the sunrise
for no reason other than
you were drunk
and you were swaying
and the blades in your clutches
were cool and reassuring
and you never felt embarrassed
for once.

remember how you felt
collected and altogether, at peace
after accepting the light at the tunnel's end
were cars speeding towards you in the night.

never let it leave, embrace it
don't let the gathering tinfoil used to keep
the crazy in
steal that memory

i remember i did it, one time

i escaped.

safety

the bins get collected tomorrow
and the cardboard needs to be
torn up to save space, or the binmen
won't take it away
and the sock that got
lost in the wash
remains unfound, a whole month
after the search and rescue
mission got started.

it escaped the screaming kids and the
traffic jams, unaffordable
student loans
and disinformation campaigns
and alarm clock cycles
sit-down-piss treats,
self-described adult
ravenclaws
and other such shit.

the routine is intact,
the chaos is at bay, but the same
can't be said for the insanity
of when the phone dies
and the music stops
and the talk of murder is fine
in restaurants, but the talk of politics
is not

none here have been
sufficiently medicated by
the spit-polished gun barrel
in the mouth
cure all

and i don't know

what any of us did
to deserve this.

the three alcoholics

three alcoholics sit on a bench outside
the bowls field on linacre road.
every morning i see them, getting angry
about things i don't quite catch

their leathery faces look heavy
and hard to lug around

every morning i watch them wear down
that withered bench
just a little more, without thinking about
the damage they're doing to it.

blackbirds hang around and watch them too,
on the telephone wires
waiting in earnest,
just in case their vomit contains some
intact food.

the people waiting for jobs to ring in
at the best pizza place in bootle,
they watch them too;
they do it in the evening
when i'm on the bus home.

they seem to have an endless supply of booze
but no sympathy at all comes their way

they're free,
they're not cowards
like us.

but i wonder if they know
just how free they are.

heebie's basement

my fingernails are getting too long
and this whole place smells of
fragile cock
and too much failing cheap cologne,
and the walls weep
until everybody goes home.

i have missed this place
i don't feel so ugly in the basement
when the smoke machine pisses
and i can smell
what i want

in the basement
all the eyes don't watch me
in the basement;
all the blooms are
pointless, because we
all sound the same
look the same, sweat the same
in the basement
and my cock
doesn't smell fragile

that's reassuring, i think
i could
waste my time
in worse ways,
watching the hands
on a clock
circle
hour after hour
feel them stab into my nape
burst the pulses
strangle me.

1 hour
60 mins

my fingernails are too long.

toilet

the king was never really
an inspiration of mine
and i never thought much
of his thrown
yet here i am, imitating him
dead on a toilet
in a blinding white cubicle,
waiting
for home time
or for the office phone
to summon me back
to the uncomfortable chair that
doesn't have armrests
(they're a fire hazard, apparently)

it's adorned with
new and old smears of
somebody else's blood,
and little puke nuggets

i don't shit in public, and all my colleagues know it

what if it smells?
what if all those prying nostrils
finally suss the reality from the
dirty protests
i've circularly scrawled
over the years?

i am not who i am,
i am a blend of the procreated thoughts
of what others make me

i want to stay here
forever
where only

the clever mathematics and
silicon valley staff
know me

but sadly
my battery will die
before i do.

optimism for the modern age

on the rain-glossed pavement
a tent, decorated with
palm tree silhouettes
against a sunset backdrop
bellows in the wind
outside the shiny lord street branch
of hsbc.

an addict is
alive or dead
in there,
but schrödinger's cat
is what matters.

the prostitutes of sheil road

they're forgotten by everybody, left to fend for themselves
but that's not my problem, i told one of them
as her scant c-cup and polluted legs
jittered around the passenger seat
of my beamer.

she whistled something through the gaps in her teeth,
darkened gums almost bleeding

that's poor life choices coming back to haunt you
i advised
subsidise your losses, get a crisis loan from the dole
while it's still around
i know you're charging me over the odds,
because i saw a woman charge four-fifty
for a blowy
it was on the bbc, part of their
poverty porn series.

her mangled talking grew louder and
increasingly desperate as the rundown streetlights
whimpered on,
she could hardly look at me, just gesticulate
wilder and wilder

i yielded , told her that she's
a bit prettier than
the other ones i watched
walk along there that night,
that's why i picked her,
but looks didn't ultimately
bother me too much, i said
this was about me
and my cock
and her slobbering on it

the market's hands are invisible
unlike mine, and i would have taken what i wanted
if push came to shove.

she continued on and on, clearly
misunderstanding the point

we must have spat for a good half an hour
until i informed her
that i was out to tender
and that it was my offer or nothing, since
the lowest bidder wins, and that i
would happily go elsewhere.

she had kids to feed
an addiction to sustain
again, that was not my problem
and i told her as such, advised her
she just needs to work harder

this went on, and the temperature dropped
she shivered, and gave in to reason

it was a good suck, i'll give her that.

all's well that ends well.

£4.50
30 mins

black umbrellas

businesspeople
run around
in the rain;

dark suits and
black umbrellas
keep their woes
nice and dry, instead of letting
the droplets
wash them away.

these days

not knowing
seems to be sinful
these days.

into pieces

i am cut to pieces
as You can tell,
golden little pieces,
and scared of not knowing
what gentle butterfly nets
will catch me, to what cemetery
the cooling breeze
will drag me

i'd ask You
to gather me up
in a heap, and char me

but You made me this way,
cut around me
into me,
chopped me up, and decided
i'm not good enough

so You can do what You want
with me now, take every last
fucking fragment
and feed me to the animals
if You really want to.

i can't stop You;
i could never take Your hands off me

not You
not Your
midas touch.

late

i was always
fashionably late;
my goth phase
never started until
my late teens.
in fact, the last time
i came early to anything,
i was prematurely ejaculated

and i'm late again,
at least it feels that way, K,
since the opportunity
to escape in You
has passed,
and i was so close to freedom
i could taste You,
so close to hope
i could feel Your hands circle
around my neck;

late / early

but it's too late
to tell You all this,
and although i will write for You,
about You, again and again,
it's only when i stand
wasting work's time
watching the golden spiral
flow down the urinal,
i realise how late
i truly am.

look up (you're being lied to)

look up
and watch the shimmering, new
looping
high-rise fingers
scratching at the clouds
while you strive
to avoid the
pavement cracks
at any cost,
as you plod
to work
or to withdraw your
last tenner
midway through the month
or stroke you hidden replica
on your way to hold up
some imaginary joint or other.

look up, do you ever
feel like you're falling?

10

bubbles

i was frozen by loss
before i lost myself
before realising that
floating away
on wabi-sabi gusts
never did anybody
any good

before realising
nothing was mine
to begin with

before knowing the walls
that circle us
only bleed us dry
and laugh as they do so.

burst the bubble
and lose yourself
burst it
and spiral down—
find the rest of us.

high enough

smoke funny things,
they'll make you laugh
and there will even be
peace on earth
when you're
high enough.

americans

americans
you are free
to do what
exactly?

are any of us really free
to do anything?

we are
where we are
because we follow
the
trend
cycle
until we spiral
uncontrollably
and wind up in one madhouse
or another

and that's terrifying

especially for americans
since all they talk about is freedom.

dreamers

stars dot
corners in the night, the ones
i turn to in my sleep

that's when i best forget
the blood rivers, watched
by the glorified
arrogant
pearly white smiles.

everything is boring

the final day off
before my leave runs out
and i have none left
until september.

the radio
is aspartame this morning. it's
asking unfunny white van men
to call in and tell
unfunny tales
about their unfunny wives
and the unfunny bad habits
they have,
and everybody
laughs about it
to fight off
genocidal urges.

sometimes a woman gets through
but her tales are also
unfunny
and this goes around
and around
and around

everybody laughs at them, too;
the urges
must be getting powerful

it's been this way for the last week
when it's too cold to tan my tits
in the garden, and too cold
to not take pictures
of my legs,
of an open beer bottle, label turned
to the lens

i'm thinking about the
lukewarm seepage
running down from my ears to where
my jawline used to be,
thinking about how
we don't judge books by their covers
but we do judge fucks by their lovers

the flies can rest in my mouth
if they want to

the radio's playing some four/four,
duh
        duh
                duh
                        duh
duh
        duh
                duh
                        duh
sounds now, and the unfunny men
are probably on youtube
self-assuring
themselves that their lives
are shit
because of people poorer than them
(the darker ones especially)

the lust for genocide
death by
happy bullets
is overbearing;

will anybody know
that i've had the week off?

4-4   7(week)

stand up (the truth)

circle back around
through time
and know
you are not permanent,
know that having
no power
is the greatest power of all

we are small, insignificant
things, in a place too big
and complicated to
fully appreciate;

you are a hubristic bug
on a freckle
that thinks it's
climbing mountains,
that thinks it knows
better, but
cannot see
the size of the hands
racing down to swat you

so enjoy
and learn to love
the little things,
because nothing
truly big
will ever happen to us.

the system (i)

i tell myself i'm
not Your prisoner anymore

all my chains are golden
so i must be free,

i'm independent;

all the money in the world
will never buy me

…

that is
until
i think of how You'd
kiss me,
until You show me how
You're still all around
yet nowhere,
and there's never any
escaping Your
unrelenting privatisation,
Your invasive marketing
Your pseudo-sentimental sensationalism,
the beautiful indoctrination of Your
talking head, the only one
we both want me to see.

we both want me to think
i can fuck the system;
You sell me as much to keep me warm
and that lie does;

i keep hoping

i can
fuck You,
but You know
i never will.

the system (ii)

these are the thoughts that set
fire to Your cities;

and i know the system is fixed,
and i know You don't want me
to break it
so i'm made to love You instead,

—and i do love You

i only love You
because You tell me to
and i don't know any better,
or any way to square this circle

i am surrendered
rendered legally tender, caratless
and there's no escaping
You

You,
the one i'd
blindly follow
around the clock,
fall off this earth
face first,
blindly stay
and never leave
You,
blindly believe
Your
cancerous
yellow ribbons
over my own
convictions.

the heart

the heart takes you down
an uncountable number
of paths, a labyrinth of itself,
when it hits
the frozen soil
and shatters,

then it leaves you there
to figure out what goes where
without
cutting yourself open
when you can't
comprehend
why it ever happened
in the first place,
when you're lost
and you can't fix it
and you just want to
skip to the end
because that's where
the good bits are—

but when you're lost
is when you feel
most alive.

smoking kills

linger here
cling to me
flow in the dim
evening light
ghostly hues
help me breathe
encircle me
for the night

subtle notes
thick as ink
kill me softly
at my lips
my fingertips
whispering
these dirty words
at your hips

i am yours
you are mine
every kiss
pulls the sky
the fire burns
and you rise
slowly recline
watch me die;

make the smoke
piss out of me.

blindfolds

keep secret
the bruising wakes
illicitly
ebbed on your
surfaces,
screaming out
against
your dripping sands,
when you're bound
in twitching chains
helpless,
capitulated
drenched in the dead night
blindfolded
and gagged
and choking in
my bare hands
with a wide and trembling smile

we can't speak of
your rattling bones
our scorched friction
and our guttural
undertones
carved into you
with my teeth,
cutting into you
like my embedded fingerprints do,
pulled out by my mouth,
forced out by my invasion

the sinful candlewax
rolling on your areola
the crops and the latex and that oil that
makes your ass glow
all of it

must be put back
where no eye can see
and my fistful of your blasphemous
dripping hair,
will stay clenched
forever

we fuck like
endangered animals
goners
in our own private
dimmed corner
dogged and primal, shrouded in
evaporating sweat
and salivating libidos
with which we decorate the room

nobody can ever know
what we do
in the darkness,

we must take our love
bound and crushed
to the grave—

like the cold fusion
that
never
happened.

divine

yes.
my vision is tinted
gold,
my love for You does not stop,
it burns, it spirals out
eternally;
there is no escaping it

this love, it never ends.

eclipse

reporters say total eclipses are rare
but they're wrong

total eclipses are visible
every eighteen months
somewhere on earth

perception makes the eye
and the ego
the centre of the universe

but we don't
take others
into account

because only
we exist.

18 months

die later

constellations
and their covalent bonds
are the foundations
i'm built on

the galaxy is full
of my twinkling molecular
compounds

and i spiral
throughout both

they're one in the same,
the universe
my nerves and my veins

i know that i will die later,
my dilator;
i look forward to being
my past self
there with you
again.

birdshit

the seagulls and pigeons are good
they can do no wrong

the seagulls are braver now,
and the pigeons still
snap their necks
flying into translucent high-rises,
never learning not to

sometimes pigeons survive
the city long enough
to eat crumbs and dust
and tear open
half-eaten sandwiches
left in questionable, violent smudges
in the abandoned
shop entrances
on church street
and bold street
and whitechapel,
before the seagulls come
and take what they please
if they can't
snatch some candy
from straight out
of an adult's hand

the seagulls are bigger than
the pigeons,
and they get away with murder
while the pigeons are called vermin,
and the upstanding
white doves
can forgot about their
darker cousins
and their sufferings

sometimes the pigeons get
their own back
when a truck or bus crushes
a seagull, mashing it
into the tarmac,
but not before many pigeons
suffer the same fate

they have no higher ideals
they pretend to care about,
they just do

hounds don't care that they're
disembowelling foxes for sport,
crocodiles don't care
about drowning
the only adolescent
zebra left in the herd,
and the mosquitoes don't care
about malaria

the hairdresser i'm sat with
is nice enough, chatty
in a typical way
but she's cutting it wrong again
and i'm going to look like
an undescended testicle
for weeks,
but i'll still tip her
careful not to cause a fuss

at least the birds don't pretend,
they just shit as they please.

fishing

giving a man
a fishing rod
doesn't help
when all the fishes
are gone,
when you take
all the fishes
away
in big ships
that empty
the sea.

christmastime and other bleak periods

a local man got his
picture taken
in a local paper
on a death-rattle
christmas eve,
when he weighed six stone
with his ribs
and his backbone on show
for all the people
looking the other way
to see.

the money he needed
for his food
was stopped

it was paid back later, though
but he still couldn't get food
because his family used the money
to bury him instead

and a woman died, desperate and
alone in a tent
at thirty years of age
not long before

and a squaddie starved
with spare change in his bank account
the job applications at his bedside
his only company

and a woman dressed in knee-high boots
was curled up outside a jewellers,
with police at her side
and a circle around her,
her makeup unmoving

the guy
with the chirpy grey dog
wasn't there like usual,
maybe she'd nicked his spot
or something,
and her makeup
attracted more attention

i didn't stop to find out.

the addicts are just addicts
and the poor are just poor
and the plastic bags
are just plastic bags
at least she was somebody.

don't come crying to us

throw all the bones you want
to the war-wolves,
starve yourself of morality
if you like,
just to make your friends
that little bit richer.
but when
the wolves of war
turn and behold
your bones
don't come crying to us.

luckies are less irritating

it's staggering to think that
the people who oppose
abortion the most
are the people that would
drop everything,
and leave the house,
to buy cigarettes
if they never planned
on being a father.

jillboots can kill a man

i have tried
for year after dumbfounded year
to ascertain
why men are more equal
than the women that make us

and still i have no idea
why men seek dominance
over equality
followers over partners,
obligations
and control,
head at the dining room table
over eating out

i cannot explain
why the fat ones don't matter
and the thin ones don't matter
and the ugly ones don't matter,

and the ones with minds of their own,
they matter the least

only the sad ones
with open dms;
they're the only ones
that matter

i don't understand why
the men that make the laws
speak for vaginas
and not themselves

men speak for a woman's body
and what to do with it

i can't explain away
the surge in beatings
every time the national footy team loses

the only possible reason
i can deduce is:
men are terrified of women

they're terrified that women
will outshine them
or kill them while on their periods and
get away with murder
which is easily done.

men know it
and that's the best explanation i have.

all you need know

you don't need permission
to smile and illuminate this earth

you don't need to
justify your power

you know you keep us
on track; you know you
keep us alive

you are the star
that ends
all the darkest nights
and ushers in all days
when the light pollution breaks,

not just when one sky
says so himself.

stones

i spend my days
extinguishing
the still-lit stubs
of Your name
on my tongue

until it ties itself up
and writhes,

until it is torn up
as i cannibalise
those golden
acetone words
and cradle the knots
they forge
in my gut.

they say names
will never hurt you,
but in my belly,
Your name
sticks;
it stones me
until my
bones break.

fuck you

all you dumb fucks
yeah you,
dumb fuck,
looking for
quick and easy
piggies
to take to market
to sell
to other
dumb fucks,
you are killing
all that is sacred;

you are to blame
for when
the world
ends
without
a
bang.

before the devil knows i'm dead

give me an hour
in heaven
before the devil
knows i'm dead

just an hour away from
money that inks the oceans
away from the felled tree limbs
selfishly taking up
too much of my room

away from carbon dioxide stranglehold
plastic hearts covered in shiny plastic sequins
oily palms and gym selfies
nicotine patches, and limbless kids
and dirty cars with dirty exhausts
coltan mined by slaves
uranium-powered cock fantasies
smokestacks

all the colourless egg cartons
in the sunday morning trollies
of the indifferent cadavers

give me just an hour
to sleep
before i have to
look in the mirror
and go to work.

old thoughts and new thoughts

nobody would get dressed,
even though at that time of morning
formby beach is freezing, and the sand
really whips against you
and it gets in all your hair
and clogs the bathroom plugs up
for days afterwards;

one of the naked people had shaved
his pubes especially,
kept his hat on too, as he always did
(such was the fashion for goths at the time)
a woollen beanie, what we used to call johnny hats,
since they looked like well-used condoms
that were just a little too big,
and the people in them
looked like dicks.

he was naked and happy, even though he was
surrounded by naked straight boys,
and he was straight too,
and the girls were sensible
and got dressed hours ago;
he was immune to the sand
so myself and a few others
filled his doc martens with sand
and pissed in them
so he came down to our level.

that was back when there was meaning, and misery
was just a mild convenience
widely understood,
and a long wait for the first train home
in clothes covered in exploded spray paint,
stinking of illegality and cheap cider

i had sex that night,
and i saw all the stars bending around me
for the first and last time
but the sand got in more places than ever.

ah, old misery
i miss you.

trash

there's a still, one-legged
homeless man
trapped by the wind this morning
rustling on cracked paving slabs
besides an ornamental heap
of spent cigarette-ends stubbed out by
welting
almost deranged office workers

his empty wheelchair is next to him;
dunno where his itchy blanket is,
the cops probably took it
when they shooed him away
from the benches outside the courts.

that's when lots of no-longer-useful people
blew away

he's less ill-fit
than the rushing drainpipe slacks
trimmed to within an inch of their lives
marching along the mall this morning

their bosses must be pleased

a lady tells me
this person
throws things at those passing by
as she adds her coffin nail
to the pile.

that was her only concern.

on equal fuckings

i'm a scrounger
to you

i would eat you alive
if i could.

we can still fuck, though;

we could have the best fuck
of our lives.

then we are
no longer different.

alpha

only the caged wolf
tries to dominate
the wolves around him
by proving how much more
of a wolf
he is
than the others.

as above, so below
i suppose.

opium

slip
far away
slide away on
 overboard soap suds

blame them,
sting them up
they are the real witches, the tv says
not us,
blame them

chase goosey, the tv says
chase goosey all around
goosey, goosey, have a gander
they're coming after you,

this will make it better;
sit in the kitchen doorway
foetal and
at a loss
and wait.

sodden rags float
face down

guess they were
innocent
after all.

lol

from an early age
i concluded i'm
the only fleshy human
in existence
and all the other people
are androids,
npc androids,
filled with wires
and perfectly round cogs,
no blood
or
humour,
dotted about the place
to bother me.

the longer i live
the more i realise
how right i was.

title: wewwo.mfvcnw page: one hundred and eight

there is a library that exists,
where you can type any
three thousand two hundred character passage
that comes to mind, even the
ping pong thoughts in your head, like this

blah blah blah this is not poetry it is pooetry, ha ha ha i made you
waste your money die die die.

you will get an exact match. it is called
the library of babel, and it contains
every line in every book
ever written, and every line in every book
that could ever be written.

wait a minute...

cracks

you are the centre of your own universe
and you construct
your own world, and you build
your own house
using the materials and tools
given to you,

and if the wood is damp and rotted
build the house anyway
and get to know that stink

if you don't have running water
build the house anyway
and know the dirt,

and if you don't have panes for windows
build the house anyway
and sit in the dark

and when you grow tired of the stink
the dirt
the dark,
snap
lash out
until you split your skin
and fracture your spirit
lash out
enough to crack the wood open
because light pierces those cracks,
and they're the cracks we all try to
wallpaper over.

i

try.

i try

so damn hard

to fight my way out

of Your all-encompassing
gold

but Your fundamental sequences
are everywhere,

replete
ubiquitous
no matter
where i turn;
Your presence is
all around

and it never stops enveloping me
in Your unrepentant appetite,
burning me alive
in Your kaleidoscopic churchyard fire.

Your golden inferno found my centre
and thus my spiralling began;
between great waves and flower heads
i lost all the illusions of my control
to believe in You
and love You,
even if all this is
just a coincidence.

the war

no war
killed more, spilled more blood
than the war
of everyday existence
in the shadows of greats
and in the pocket of
everything else

movies aren't made
about that war
or the people that die
in it,
no;
that war doesn't have
hired guns that kill
to become heroes, it
just has people.

some become villains
and end up dying
for that
new house, new car
new bathroom suite
that looks just a little different
than the last one,
but maybe the
two and a bit kids will
give a damn about this one

some die rich
with fancy
new wartime watches
for their collections

they're the villains trying
to buy more time

as the sucker punch
of a life spent
running in circles
chasing profit
finally hits home

their rolexes may be
timeless and shine brighter
in the phlegmy dusk, but truly
priceless things
like time
aren't worth
all that much
to them now

the real heroes
reside in the silence of
half-full bottles of wine
at their bedsides
in which
they wish to drown,
they fight
and fuck
and love on some days
and cry on others;
they are incorruptible and
unafraid to admit
their sadness
when it's not
international mental
health day,
when people who
don't understand
don't pretend they do.

real heroes, instead,
die in the night
unconcerned
about the villains

that surround them.

or maybe i'm just feeling
sorry for myself.

all that glitters

You threw down the penny
and i'm still begging for the
blistering clang to deafen
the globe,
i'm still clinging onto it
fooling myself into thinking
i'm worth my weight to You

and i still have no clue
that i'm spinning downwards
out of control
holding onto my own
fool's gold

maybe i'm dizzy and just
kidding myself;
maybe the penny hit the bottom
and maybe the bottom is better than being
out of control, up in the air
where the friction scalds

You're heavier than my emptiness
and a centre for me to cling
and You're still mine in my mind

that will comfort me
whatever the outcome
whether i'm at the bottom
or not.

sitting outside

i drink
and the sun empties
skimmed milk
cartons
on my face, and
i stand up
scratch,
then sit again
for something to do.

i can't remember
what i came here
for
if anything at all
so i drink, thinking
to myself
about how real people
only see
champ, never
pain

they fool
themselves.

bombs

if you
put up affronts
when c-bombs drop
but remain
apathetic
when you see
bombs drop
you are a cunt.

life and soul of the party

you took away the knife he used
to start cutting us free
from the tightened belts
we hang by.

you looked him directly
in his eyes, and you jarred it
in his front,
and smiled ear to ear.

you did it for the thousandth time;
you did it, we saw
the life and soul of the party
bleed all over you.

you did it to
break him as a man
you did it knowing how we'd suffer
in our millions
knowing we were watching
knowing we know.

but we remember.
we always do.

here

the riots continue in france;
or do they?
the tv hasn't told me about them
in a while

maybe that's why
we make excuses here?

yeah, we jump through hoops
here
we don't blame anything on
the rich here
we just let the people starve
here
freeze
here
sleep on the roadside
here;

we keep calm and carry on
here;

we blame the victims
blame the poor
blame the brown people
blame the women
blame the immigrants
here,

but there are protests
in hong kong
and russia.

boiling frogs

frogs hop out the pan
when the water
gets warm

it's a myth that they do nothing.

the only frog to have been
cooked alive
was lobotomised

humans, on the other hand,
knowing they're boiling alive
turn up the gas.

live longer

live longer,
do as you're told
slow down, idiot
pay attention at work

don't speak
don't ever leave bed
don't fuck me
count the rebellious hairs
on the pillow
in silence

i don't miss you,
just the idea of
having you around

focus on our
proprioception
acquiesce, be trapped
in the ignorance
fake a smile
to fake people
on fake occasions
stabilise me
and my all-over-the-place demeanour

guzzle your analgesics
and your antiseptics
be squeaky-clean
please stop falling down
don't ever fall in love
you'll end up all emotional

choose the safety of bars on your windows
and the reassuring barrel
of a shotgun at the base of your spine

as an egg timer
sits lonely
talking to itself
pointlessly
pulling
at string.

live a longer life
brought to us by:
the law of cosmic laziness.

until my head falls off

#prayforparis
#prayforlondon
you'd better get on your tweets
and #prayforbrussels
i laugh until my head falls off
we never #prayforyemen
or #libya
or #iraq
or #afghanistan

i wish they'd show
where the missiles land
on tv.

hurry up
tell us the ethnicity
i must respond accordingly
is it a terrorist?
or is he a lone nut?
is it extreme?
or is he mentally ill?
i laugh until my head falls off
hurry up and say if i can
blame islam or not
can i blame it or not?
i need a scapegoat

i wish they'd show
mutilated hollow bodies
on the tv

will we even light up our buildings
in half-arsed attempts
to lie to ourselves
and pretend we care?

no, the bombs will continue to drop
and a vest will go off
and the bombs will drop
and a vest will go off.
get your phones out.

fuck you too

i see your gears turning
cities building, others crying
your streetlights flashing
your stomachs churning

your innards lining the powerless,
the foreign
the animals
the forests
in the boring peacetime,
while you plot to lock us out

plot to force your will
on those who choose to
run from the circles of a
bloodied
boot
kicking down their door,
plot to justify agony
and
strife,
plot to make it harder
plot to ignore the starvation
of a child
every ten
fucking
seconds.

fuck you.

come friendly robots

you know, we're the only species
arrogant and self-important enough
to deem ourselves worthy of wiping ourselves out,

but when the friendly robots come
and take our jobs
and put us in our places
outdo us in every possible way
humble us,
that's when i'll be happy.

when we finally admit
that they're better than us
and the things that dictate
what we live and die by
that's when i'll be free again
because we're obsessed with
keeping things exactly as they are,
capitalism is here forever
people change, and when they do
we try to ignore them
because we're that into ourselves
that we want to live forever
in the same place
at the same time
with nothing ever changing

and if the friendly robots come and start
going door to door, killing us all
maybe we'll finally understand that we have
no right to be here

i can only hope that they do.

da da da da da

you
spent
moments
of
your
life
reading
this
shit.

the theory of everything

her sharp edges formed
tetrahedrons that built me
and the symbiotic times
time itself
moves through
in planck length
stills.

she cast shade down
she created a holy
symmetry of
golden polytopes, and i
remain the shadow of her shadow,
a quasicrystal,
still moving
through planck length pixels,
just a fraction of the shape
no brain on earth
fully understands,

but when we blistered
we kissed, and even now
she spins me
she flavours me,
colours in my
warring relative and
quantum juxtapositions,
ceaselessly loops
the influences of my past
and my future
onto me here, now
and my eternity

the gravity
of her glances
no brain on earth

can explain,
but no brain on earth
matters.

we were the sublation of
science and spirit
conscious mathematics
in matrixes
and she flamed
golden,
her own
creation.

we vibrated freely
through each other
and all i know
emerged

but this is just
what i alone think
even to this day, as
i'm melting
in the binary sunlight

all this is just what i see
in my subjective head
and i don't know lies
from reality.
if i tell You i do,
i'm lying.

i just feel it
even if it isn't real
i feel it
shaking me
on those sexless, fatal nights
guzzling determinism
as my mandala
waves when the door closes.

all i ask of You
is to look me dead
in my double slit
and end it.

acne

all the old ones left scars,
the new ones will, too
but i do not care

i still feel You in there, even after
i take the skin off
and bleed
and the burning crusts over,
so i pick the scab, flick it away
and dig again
and bleed again
and burn again
and scar again,
because i still see You here,
feel You there

the chartreuse poison
never leaves
all the boiling lumps
all the golden circles
never leave;

they only spread forever
and take over.

gilet jaunes

go on,
flood the arteries
the ventricles
the heart, the mind
scorch the whole damn thing

stain all the marble
and glaze the boutique cafes
with Your chaotic
yellow
high-vis beauty

circle it,
tear it the fuck down
from the inside,
break the ribs and lacerate
the lungs

the immune system
needs it, despite fighting back
against Your scorched earth mentality
it is ugly, atrophic.

the immune system grew cocky
and needs overthrowing.

K, answer

Your face sinks
further away
by the day,
yet You
still consume me
and my
every hour

i can't cut
You
out, and the drugs
don't work; i just have to
keep on dragging
my searing yellowed bones
along with me
until the world stops turning.

i can't fight You off

life is over now
and i'm just waiting
for it to end
now that
You're nowhere
to be found

K, answer
i don't know if You're alive
or dead anymore;
i don't care
if You continue
to gnaw away at me,
You can have me;
i'm tired and easy now
after digging holes all around
finding not the gold i seek

but the only future
i wish to avoid.

fairytale

mickey mouse lived
inside me
once upon a time,
until i smoked him out,
drank him
under a table,
dragged him
across the floor,
into the street
and mercilessly clubbed
the lying bastard
until his bones broke
and his blood ebbed
across the cobbles
outside bar cava.

he died that night
like my old school friends

and the gathering crowd
briefly smiled
…
if only.

lost angeles

i know there's nothing left at all
when you eulogise those killers
as the whole world
took aim and fired
millions of imaginary bullets
into their corpses,
one for every human those
killers were paid to murder—
one for every human being.

they burned alive
they will never die
they will live forever
haunting the halls of power
so i'll not be speaking ill of the dead
by celebrating their lives.

i know there's nothing left
at all
when he, the killer in chief
is given relief
because he opposes
all that hot air
in words alone
whilst he buys new thrones
with the taxes he saved,
scythings that send your core support
to early graves,
the guns you carve your name into
and profit by,
the bombs you vote to buy, while you cry
and wonder why you lose.

i know there's nothing left
at all
when you embrace the hawks

that have always circled you
when you serve
your corporate overlords
when you disenfranchise
half your country and leave them destitute
when you can't
even provide for them
when they're dying, but you happily
send them away
and kill them quicker
for no other reason than
because you're bought
by the profiteers of war.

there's nothing left
at all about you.

in tongues

crazy, you say
i'm not
crazy
i'm just not enslaved
by your definition of sanity

you need to step back
and sharpen the circle
step back and watch
the pyramids
burst the bubbles that
slowly kill you

but, as always
there's nobody here to
talk to; i only hear myself
singing out of tune,
wasting away, in the spare room
until the
mushroom clouds
confirm it's safe
to leave.

the drink

mouth ajar,
my head in delayed recline
tilts ever backwards
onto dried blood circles
where i won't wish i'd died
for a while,
at least until earth
stops rotating on my axis,
until these boozy strokes
no longer feel so distant.

it's a clean break
a sluggish cleave through
the vertebrae,
my blushing backdrops
can quieten for now
just while i disappear
because when reality bites,
life sucks me dry.

i'll anxiously wait
until all around me
corkscrews away.

umbra

a wino's arse is bare
his pants have fallen down
as he shuffles
off the bus
coughing his lungs up

i am on my way home
now
going to lie down

my cocaine skin is flaking off
but i don't care enough
to wash it

a wino's
arse is bare
his pants have
fallen down
and the houses
around here
look better
roughed up

i am on my way home
now
will probably
skip food

my music has stopped playing
faster than expected.

softcore

do i feel things
none of you do?
i have a feeling
that just isn't true
i'm human, just like you;
are you human
too?

i dunno

turn on the tv;
there's nothing new
to me
since the news
always seems too bad
to be true
and the sadness
shows no signs
of stopping

is that why we
ultimately
do nothing?

the thrill's
going,
going
gone.

fuck
everything.
and leave the tv on

allegory

alcohol and legs season is over, and
love is now just an
odd sock that mops up the only
spillage in an empty house,
a cave where reality crawls
the walls and ceiling
in black and white—
in the whimpering flame
of the only lighter i have

it feels like i've
been here forever, but
this isn't everything, i know
it can't be; i know i've seen
more than these
rattling duvets chaining me in place
the gnashing pipes beneath the
greasy floorboards;
the bathroom that's probably
flooded again where i sometimes
meet the maths in private. but
all this is private now
this is all there is
cold, smashed beer glass in the kitchen
laughing with the
unhinged doors and the lonely
egg timer.
no food
no third eye candy
in the pot
nothing.

i might not
make the night; i might
die later.

wonder what time it is;
the sun's been gone
for a while now. there's blackness
and war outside
no heads bobbling over
the pits in the pavement; the
birds have shit on next door's
car, and she's going to be pissed.
shit's hard to scrape off
the windscreen when it's
this cold. at least the frog near the door
made it inside safely, unlike
the prostitutes that once gargled and spoke
to me more humanely than any
of those snarling machines; wonder if
the wabi-sabi gusts took them some place
nice, the sunset tent and wheelchairs too;
wonder if they found the lost leg, or
the dry grass heaps? they might be free,
like alcoholics sitting on a bench all day.

my lighter has finally
ran out, and the only thing left
is self-love. i must love myself

heavies might come around
in the morning; little do
they know the power
is already cut off, the phone
doesn't ring and the tv
doesn't turn on either;
there's no hot water,
dumb fucks; only big knickers
in the corner, and the
empty fish tank.
they could take the tank, but the fishes
are gone, already taken away. the water
is probably frozen over, glass
might smash when the missiles

land, the mushroom clouds might
knock it out their hands;
it will be okay then; i can leave
the cave again
leave the cold, take this biting
hat off take all these layers off
kick the duvets off
and it might stop hailing too
and i could take a piss
if that isn't frozen too.
hope the dark-gummed lady
is okay. i guess that she who gobs
the wood warms herself twice.

could be worse, could be
an unfunny wife of an unfunny
white van man

here exists nothing,
nothing nothing nothing. i've seen
what's outside, and in here
there's nothing
no fantasies in high definition
no warm water, no self-love
only a cave
full of nothing but my
imagination and memories
and they're no good now
since i don't know which
is which

i don't know if i ever
pissed smoke
or if my pubic hairs ever
had old miserable sand tangled in them.
there's no basement, all the smells
are frozen in the air, hanging
by their neckties, bloody
circles are getting louder.

i know only of my cramping body
my cramping calf, my fragile
stinging dick, bleeding sack.
it's too cold to fuse
fact and fiction together.
my brain is blindfolded
and i'm the one twitching in the steel
duvets this time; must've taken
a wrong turn somewhere in
the labyrinth and twisted around
back to near the beginning, got lost.
is this what being alive
feels like? i don't know, probably
punishment for my sins.
(love myself love myself
love myself some more)

but i can't; my cherished love
is hardened, has holes in it
now. and after escaping the screaming kids
and the traffic jams, this is what
it came to. the marrow
of my bones
is shaking so much
it's making my spirit bleed.
the self-love stopped coming
a while ago, i have nothing more
to give. it's icy and the closed-throat pain
the tectonic pummelling
the slow fingering pangs
smash my core
and it's still
dark outside. the dreamers
will be smiling at least
no blood spilt for them; they have
all the toilet paper
they desire; i've used
all mine.

i can't tell a soul; they might
kill me if i do. i might die later
if i tell anybody

light lets us see what darkness made

but darkness isn't what they're
looking for. i guess they were
innocent, and this is punishment
after all.

hardcore

fuck this—
it's all chmess—
nothing exists;
i'm running on empty

i crossed off
my first death wish from the hundred that
occupy my kick the bucket list

i embraced death,
and will always pay more for my
morbid fascinations
than any muscle-bound state
could possibly enforce

the pen's my weapon of war
and i've been dying
to get these words out
though these red scores
across my throat
don't cut as deep as the sword

you can call it insanity if you want to
because to be considered
sane, in times this insane
is an insult,
and this truth will only become known
when you observe it,
but so few look

got sick of
having my head turned;
but now i can look back and laugh
(cue laugh track)
because it's all a tragic comedy
that so many aspire to spin towards

insentient obscurity
with a smile
while i am forced to
make beds out of
these words, and exist solely
in these pages
looping looping looping
whenever people read or misunderstand them
misunderstand everything

and i'm dead tired,
an inzombiac,
brutalised by
the absurd,
the quiet life
as the finasteride
stops me in my tracks.

pornography

if love isn't a viability
fake it for me,
i'll be deathbed-white
watching
waiting
deteriorating
as society slowly rots around me, regressing
in synchronicity with my mind
as maniacal smiles illuminate the sombre serenity
of locked phone screens
that reflect my twisted fit-throwing
while i abjure my sanity
coiled in hysteria.

shut up and dance
shut up and dance
won't you please just shut the fuck up
and dance?

fuck
i'm not normal
validate me
through appropriation;
like my pictures
comment on and share them
feed me others' misery
i'll eat it alive
because everything's for sale;
market my dissent
on t-shirts and badges
adorned
with the propaganda of hate
fuck the media
fuck the system
fuck this
fuck that,

i'm selling all my glamorous diseases
because my anti-pious lifestyle
misses the point
every
fucking
time.

but i can fart the alphabet
isn't that brilliant?
of course i'm talking
out of my arse;
like everything you choose to believe
i'm a farce
authentic
augmented
it doesn't matter,
as i am
who i am not
i solely exist in the constraints
of your truth.

eulogise me
rate me
give me pigs to fuck
vomit to swallow
as i hide
every inch of my screen-burnt mortality.

i'll never swear to you
because nothing's real anymore
and the illusion is draining
maiming my sanity
until
i give in
and revel in crass sin.

i'll nosedive
to the barrel-bottom

bespattered and bloodied
by your love.

mum

a sinkhole opened up
outside the strand—
a fitting place
for the world to start ending—
though only bus routes
are disturbed;
it's swallowed nothing
yet

i hope mum hurries, hope it grows
and drains the ever-tutting
arthritic perms
and the bricks of beirut
all the sick and all their
heroin spoons
underneath the rotting
overpass by tesco express

i want the ground to splinter and devour
rhyl's growling sun centre, drag blackpool tower down
beam by fucking beam,
send the arndale centre crashing
into the soil's loving arms
choke the bitch that robbed me
with the sludge of picadilly gardens
crush birmingham's ugly facades
and make them mangled and beautiful
at last

drop the ancient blocks at stonehenge
on the heads of
all the tourists
eat the poor and the posh of london
and all their fucking
wasted babies
consume this rotten island whole.

hope the whirlpools open
and grind up every
gleaming cruise ship
every bored child,
every submarine,
crushes the piers and
the fancy beachfront hotels
and the rich people
that stay in them
and the poor people
that work them,
send waves surging up every european river
flood the cities, flood the towns
sink the renaissance
with the sewage
humans leave behind

mum's revolution will be televised
until the fires char the anchors
and the lobbyists in dc
and the acid rain dissolves news headquarters,
the faults all gape at once, engulfing
the overpriced and shit
california mansions
of lazy hollywood executives
and landslides bury the terracotta army again
and raze the asian balenciaga sweatshops
and send machu picchu
tumbling down the fucking
mountainside.

please tidal waves
knock down
all the fucking ipanema
apartment complexes
please cyclone season come early
and rip up the smiling pagodas
all those little straw huts

on every fucking atoll
smash into the opera house
and all the dull fucks
with paper ornaments
in their cocktails

i want the lions to hunt
all the poachers on the plains
wildebeests to trample safari guides
and hippos to charge
the oglers from behind,
upturn their draconian trucks
and sandstorms to topple giza
snow to raid the seed vault
and gun down the pleading
labcoats unpityingly,
hurricanes to smash into
the caribbean tax havens
every fucking coked-up lawyer
and all their llps
the nukes weep
and vaporise every word
every fucking database
liquefy the formalists
the clever angles
rip apart the swimsuit adverts—
all of them

eruptions please erase
every fucking trace
of our existence
the dandruff, the dust
i want the sky to fall on us

please mum
hurry up,
smite us
hurry up and
smite me too

i'll be fucking smitten

these words feel like the doomsday
clock ticking down, but they're
only words in
a poem,
and the pothole
got fixed
by the time you read it.

i don't know

i'm bleeding again;
been trying to cover myself in lemon juice
until i broke the skin

i tried
and failed
to crush into my own
schwartzchild radius,
i can't fall through the encircling prismatic fractals,
be sucked into my all-seeing
stable
mandelbrot abyss
my beautiful,
imaginary accretion disks.

there's no escaping the senseless borders
we're all convinced have limits
and i'm too stupid to count
from zero to one in
real numbers
i'm told can't be proven
anyway.

i guess some infinities are just
bigger than others.

hypernormalisation

please, s/top <the car>

st[op] %ly///ing

                         we've been
         driving
me in_circles
all   day
            </>
      >
>
[&] all… life

we're not
go_ing
…
anywhere

and i
must   sepa[/]rate

split from the
discol[our]ed
torn
leat///her

seats

/ctrl+alt+del//ctrl+alt+del/ctrl+alt+del/ctrl+alt+del/

stop <the car>
binary_glitches
of these
moanings+   bitchings+
un[%]naturally white
teeth mal/fun/ction in

the m[irror]s
ill/uminate
the… c[rack]s

in the

road…side

[lie] <stop>

/just a ride/

i've gam<%bled>

never w[on]

        01001111_ O
   01101110_ N
          01100101_ E
     00100000
    /01101001_ I
01101110_ N
   00100000_
     01100001 A
       00100000_
         01100010_ B
       01101001_ I
     01101100/ L
   01101100_ L
     01101001_ I
   01101111_ O
     01101110 N

One in a billion

it's all sordid
mor>bid+hate+sex too
…

_matter_less_%

Oxytocin - Love

/C8H11NO2+C10H12N2O+C43H66N12O12S2

</the car>
</the car>
</the car>
</the car>
</the car>
</the car>
</the car>
</the car>
</the car>
</the car>

bleach

why am i here?
that's a question i've asked myself many times,
but what difference does it make?
i'm the result of twenty something years
of mistakes; deal with it
and stop watching broken clocks
trying to guess when the time is right.

though, You ought to know that
at night
the only sounds i hear
are empty pens scraping circles on yellowing paper,
cogs in my head grinding
to a halt,
because i deliberately
rubbed salt into my wounds.
i'm not as calculated as i thought
but does that matter?
i spiralled
drank bleach
hoping to be reborn
ignoring the stale blood,
starving myself of food for thought
and instead
focusing on the arylide web of worlds
at my fingertips,
by force or by choice
i don't know which,

scrambling to find what
You took from me
candy from Your baby
as i endlessly cycle
around rock n roll
cheap sex

bottle necks and tourniquets
none of which did the trick
failed to stopped the itch
i need a proper fix
the one i found in You
i don't know what to do
because i run in circles
failing every time to find You
and then waste time
wondering where life went

why am i here?
the question i ask myself
many times.

picture

this sparkling lovebird's chirping persists;
i'd wring its neck if i could

if only this sack
this bloody membrane
weren't in the way,
if its bony cage couldn't stop me;
i'm telling You, i'd wring
its fucking neck
until the screaming colours
bled into my greyscale palms
leaving them golden
like triumphant, arrogant sunflowers
that loom above me
only to regret it afterwards—
to nervously slather the remains all around
in private, my own doomed spiral,
out of people's sight and earshot—
just me, and the ever-pounding heartache
that drives me mad

am i the only one
that hears it, the broken tone
refracting and forlorn?
i doubt it, but
i fail to escape
its solitary lilt
or the fact it's mine alone
to suffer, bittersweet
like this heartbeat
that keeps me lucid,
that tips me out
my single bed
in the morning

i hope one day it shuts up

and normality can resume
one day it might,
one day

ah, who the hell am i kidding?
i lost myself a little there,
blotto on a cocktail of the grainy illusion
of unparalleled power
the conversations she and i once had
and the narrator type of sadomasochistic beatings
i dish out to prove my points

the mirror cracked me quickly
this time around
a sight as common as muck,
one i'm sick of,
black and blues,
yellowy bruises,
nothing in between nudity
and perspective
between those tiny snaps
when i lie awake at night
blinking, carving open my own spirit
with my razor-sharp wit
nobody ever seems to snag

i'm just
unchartered
and failing to lie to my soul
but that won't stop me from trying,
is this the beginning of wisdom?
i don't know or care, frankly;
don't ever quote me
on my sobriety,
but i promise You
i'm not having
drunken words with myself
waiting for the tap water to warm,
despite the half-empty pint glass

despite the rest of the beer
spilling out my mouth
tuscany and wasted.
it's cold outside
i don't want to leave

see, i've come to know
the truth: i love it—
the necessary
searing—
so does everybody else
which is why all the best songs
are sad ones
the only difference is: i can't sell it as good
because i'm duplicitous and wasted;
spent too many discontented days
trying to strangle metaphorical birds
to notice i locked myself away,
i've walled myself in, and they're drained
and so thoroughly bored of all this futility
they've stopped responding to my inquiry
again

it's high-time i realised
the sands
i clutch for with both hands
aren't mine to hold
i'll never be in control
of the tide, so i guess
i must drift on
like it, loathe it—

that's something i'll never do
because You're the only birdsong
i can't drown out
so i'll conform, practice the smile
before braving the rain
and continuing to say
the same fucking cliché:

i'll die for You

only now,
i don't hear You say it back,
something i'm still not used to

i found what i love, see
and it killed me,
as i've said repeatedly;
i lie down,
over a puddle at the roadside
then each tender step of Yours
tore me, gutted my virility
into smithereens
with every thought, dream
every romantically sickening,
stereotypically soppy
intangible experience
a badly burnt boy
can stomach

i just hope that the gutter i die in
leaves me with
a smile on my face
after the uneventful life
the television at my bedside
tries to convince me
i'll never have

i write my own
yellow journalism
i am my own
propaganda minister

i tried to do what You said to
pressed the barrel to my head
and pulled;
the bang, almost took my eye out
and i guess

that's the difference
between us:
the cheap flag gag
and the real deal,
You have the unsolvable problems
that i lust after
because they're exciting and dramatic,
because i found myself in You
and i'm only trying to see
what Your eyes do
as they still burn in me
from way back when
You looked my way

You said the future is in Your
control;
You said You had to suffer alone;
You are the bigger flame
out of the two of us
and You suck the air
that i need—
but i'd much prefer
You to have—
since You're the supernova
we'd all like to see,
the flash of my life,
the detonation in my head
when i try to sleep,
sunshine
in wintertime
like a spirit guiding me
out the house,
You're the yellowcake lines
i cut up
on a smeared glass table
and snort
to help me fission
and forget who i am
to give me

little fragments of You;
Your dead, flaked-off skin
is better than nothing at all
and i feel as though
humanity invades me
only to take You away
and raze me, not knowing
i'll level myself
eventually

the warbling's
so soulful
the sole sounds
echoing in my inner firestorms
are what i want;
they sound precisely like You
but more distant
than countenance allows

love was such a simple thing
until You loved me
until the autopsy results
came in

just grab a hold of me
cut of my circulation—
choke me
for my own sake;
please, i want You
to put an end to my breathing
like we planned
when we fell into each other,
when You could've killed
this fucking lovebird
and prevent any
fictional ramblings such as this; instead
You made it louder, made it
screech so powerfully
i'm humbled

by my own torture,
and now i've reached the point
were i can't determine
the story from the facts

You destroyed me
and now this is who i am,
verbally naked, torrid
love or leave me,
and i can't even face it alone anymore
i can't articulate it well enough
or paint it a worthwhile gold

so You'd better draw
Your own conclusions,
they're worth a thousand
of my words.

wanker

man up,
dickhead,
you're not supposed to say this

even if it's true
even if you feel it
even if
after all
your attempts to suppress it
are futile
even if you are devout
and remain pious
forever

and ever
and ever

even if the circle
you run around is
inescapable
and your heels crust over
split, and bleed

even if you keep on running
until you expose the bone
you are a man
and men do not
say
this
shit—
ever.

Your dog

it's almost
midday
in summer
and i'm waiting for You
in Your locked car
submitted
coiled
parched and dry,
ready to die
alone
hoping that
soon, You will come back
and take me home,
You will come back
and throw me Your bones,
throw me something,

anything;

i need You to,
because i can never leave,
even if i wanted;
all i can do is sit here
still waiting
hoping that You
come back soon

but still i wait,
desolate and ragged
tail-wagged
slowly being boiled
by the golden sunbeams;

there's no place
i'd rather be.

poetry

—poetry always
highlights that,
in the end,
even full glasses are
emptied.

in storms

you can survive for three weeks without food
three days without water
three hours without shelter;

but you will not survive
for a second
without hope

never lose it;

spiral with it.

keep going;

recurring themes + motifs

time, passing of time

Love, loss, alienation, suffering, penance

political themes

stars, gravity, relativity

androids, computers, binary, screens

War of everyday existence - war in general

Rebellion

acknowledgments:

K, You are the reason this book of this. despite everything, i owe you thanks for the inspiration. aleesha, you have been a hero of mine for a long time, and the days when you used to buzz when i sent you poems pushed me on. thank you. amelia, you were there in the very early days, and it would not have happened if you hadn't encouraged me. miriam, you dealt with my shit from early on, and you watched me grow throughout the years, and i owe you a lot for that. darren and lewy, you kept me hungover enough to write this and have been my only social life for a long time, and i am eternally thankful. mum and dad, thank you for giving me the space and time of day to write this. john and kerry for not being the stereotypical annoying siblings, thanks. veronica, for giving my arse a kicking. harriet, thank you for being a day-to-day inspiration and confidant. sarah, for giving me a boost during the hello poetry days. chunk, thank you for putting a smile on my face no matter what. jade, thank you for discovering me on my little insta page and helping me grow too, and for having the cutest little life and being hilarious about it, and for editing this, too; i am beyond grateful for that. becca, thank you for helping me spread in canada and the states. becks, for helping me improve my writing and writing brilliant books to read, and being immeasurably supportive. rach, you are another person that helped me believe in myself; thank you (and thank you for the quote too). canadian madison, you are a huge inspiration to me, and the things you have achieved are what has kept me going. madison from san diego, for being hilarious and helping me think about touring and making me continue writing when i wanted to give up.sarah, for reading an atrocious first draft and still allowing me to quote you. simon, for giving my fragile ego a massive boost. shannon, again, for flattering me with your far too kind words about my work. meg, for helping guide me through the baffling world of microsoft software and giving me your priceless advice! there are countless others that would take me a lifetime to list—the people with whom i work, with whom i have come to know on twitter, instagram, and all other social media—you all know who you are; you are the people i have spoken to, put up with me, shared me, worked with me, and you have all been the most supportive people for the longest time. the world is going to shit, and you have all given me so much hope that goodness will prevail, that every daily horror will end, and i cannot possibly thank you enough. but, after all this, if you take anything away from this, know that i am eternally grateful.

recommended reads:

rebecca rijsdijk
- you were married when i met you
- the lady from across the sea
- portraits of girls i never met
- the care home (coming february 2021)

matthew haigh
- death magazine

madison gonzales
- dear mirror

guy debord
- the society of the spectacle

jean paul sartre
- no exit

jean baudrillard
- simulacra and simulation

albert camus
- the myth of sisyphus
- la peste
- the stranger

noam chomsky
- manufacturing consent

robert tressell
- the ragged trousered philanthropist

alex haley
- the autobiography of malcolm x

about the author:

michael 'mickey' finn is a writer from liverpool, uk. he has spent his entire adult life writing and has kept numerous blogs that have been read upwards of 300,000 times around the world. even throughout his childhood, he has had a fascination with words; he remembers sitting by the three-bar electric fire writing stories on tiny booklets his mother made for him. that encouragement is what kept the fire alive, and having failed to learn to properly read and properly write throughout school, he spent his late teens and early twenties, throughout the 2008 economic collapse and an unemployment crisis, poor and unemployed, teaching himself to read and write, until he—at last—beat this book out of himself. there is more to come.

instagram: @mfinnpoetry
for all enquiries, please email: mikey.finn@hotmail.co.uk

Printed in Great Britain
by Amazon

66459012R00090